STORIES

of the

Good Old Days

Rodney H. Chow

The photo shown on this book cover is my youngest sister when she was about three or four years old. The house in the background was our neighbor's. It was on Ninth Place, a half block from San Pedro Street, Los Angeles Ca. Our fish and poultry store was on the corner of Ninth Place and San Pedro Street.

STORIES OF THE GOOD OLD DAYS

Print ISBN: 979-8-35093-046-7
eBook iSBN: 979-8-35093-047-4

STORIES

—— of the ——

Good Old Days

Rodney H. Chow

EXCERPTS TO
WET YOUR CURIOSITY ABOUT THIS BOOK

Chapter 2—CHILDHOOD MEMORIES
The old neighborhood back in the 1940's

The wooden garages in the back were built back-to-back from the garages on the other side of the block and side-to-side creating a roof top of a playground for us. Boy, was that neighbor mad when he saw us running over his garage roof. He was afraid we could cause leaks on his roof. It didn't stop us. He wasn't around all the time. Whenever he was, there were those angry words. Then we hurried away rushing back to Robert's yard.

Chapter 10—OUR HERO
This is a conversation between three boys about the ten-year-old that stole his father's car key and drove his father's pickup truck in the neighborhood

"Harry drove his father's pickup truck. I saw him alone behind the steering wheel."

"Wow!" Said Jimmie. "You mean he was really driving?"

"Yep! I saw him in that truck" said Johny. "He drove the truck. The truck didn't drive him."

Chapter 12—WATTS RIOT
My learning experiences

Some of the Black men began to speak up and many listened. I was one of them. It began to impress me, especially when they exclaimed. "We do not want you to tolerate us. We want to be part of your life. Do not just laugh at our jokes, laugh with us."

This event exposed me to a very important learning event. I began to understand humanity. I learn that the most important lesson of my life was not the Watts Riot but how my Black co-workers felt.

Such is life when we were young

All we knew was today

What more do we need?

When our happiness need not extend

No farther than the day is long

Contents

FOREWORD

WE OLDSTERS NEED AN AUDIENCE TO HELP US relive the best times of our lives.

This book is a collection of short stories about growing up in an ethnic neighborhood. It is intended to let you experience our good old days. The focus of these stories is the last half of the Great Depression and the beginning of a new post war era.

Some of these stories are based on memory and some are fiction made from actual events I remembered. These short stories are about growing up in the vicinity of San Pedro Street across the street from the Los Angeles City Market from about 1938 through the 1970's. Today, some call this area another Chinatown. I disagree. I know. I grew up there. The neighborhood was a blend of Asians, Hispanics, White folks and a few Blacks. These short stories are about people who were not the descendants of the early pilgrims. They are the families that came here for a new life of freedom. They are the citizens that make up what is America today, the mix of blended America.

As I look back to those days, I see America's greatest generation. Learning to live without. Kids did it. That background (the Depression) created successful adults. They built a new life from the chaos caused by bank failures and businesses closing down

INTRODUCTION

AUTHOR'S FAMILY HISTORY IN AMERICA

This is the story of my mother's side of the family. This version of our family history, the Li family, was written by my cousin Stacy Li as told to him by his mother Augusta Li.

This is a reproduction of that history written by my cousin Stacy Li.

13th Generation – Our Great Great Grandfather: Li Chee Tai (meaning support)

We have been told that our Great Great Grandfather (Chee Tai) was the first of our ancestors to reach America. Mom said Chee Tai was working on the railroad (1860's), but that does not make sense because that occurred after the gold rush (1850's) and his son was the gold prospector. The time Chee Li was supposed to be in America would be before the acknowledged immigration of Chinese.

One day Li Chee Tai was herding ducks in the village. A foreigner came along and knocked his huge bamboo hat off with a stick. He probably stared at the foreigner, picked his hat up and continued on. Then it happened again and again. Finally, he was tested beyond his endurance.

He recognized that it was an act of hostility instead an accident because it was done repeatedly to irritate him. He was so angered that he gave chase to retaliate. It was then that Chee Tai was captured and shanghaied by the foreigner. He was taken by boat to America and thus became the first of our ancestors to reach the beautiful country (America). America in Chinese is May Gwok, beautiful country.

He must have been young. Much later, Chee Tai discovered himself in Oregon. He had jumped over board and swam ashore and lived with a Native-American women for a time, who bore him a son.

Then he returned to China, becoming a sojourner.

14th generation – our Great Grandfather: Li Hin (Meaning revelation) Chew (Meaning Era or Dynasty)

LI Chee Tai sent his son Li Hin Chew, the eldest of three sons, to America to look for his Native American "wife" and son. Unfortunately, Li Hin Chew was not successful in his search.

By this time the California Gold Rush was a reality. The Chinese called California "Gold Mountain." This places him in the 1850's. Chee Tai found a very rich deposit in gold dust. But failed to recognize it as such. He was expecting gold in the form of gold nuggets, so he didn't file his claim. This allowed another miner to file the claim. Fortunately for us, this miner's claim was jumped and he died over it. So, if Great Grandfather recognized the value of his strike, we would not be here.

Later in the 1860's, Chee Tai worked on the construction of the Central Pacific Railroad over the Sierra Neveda. He was a member of a black powder gang blasting granite barriers out of the way. The sheer cliffs of Cape Horn near Colfax, California was one location where he worked.

He returned to China as a successful sojourner having acquired enough wealth to build a Great House in the village.

Hin Chew's father (Li Chee Tai) passed away when Hin Chew was four years old. (*He had charged his four-year old son to find his older brother in Oregon?*), so he, therefore, lacked the opportunity for an extensive education. In spite of the limited education he received, he was able to read, though not at a scholarly level, and was skilled in calligraphy.

Hin Chew was a baker, and wrote a volume of recipes (wedding cakes, etc.) that he passed on to his son, Li Bing Lum. His recipes were the result of years as a diligent artisan, his calligraphy was excellent, and he gave the book to his son with great pride saying. "No matter where you're going to live, this volume of recipes is an assurance of security. You will always be able to make a living and your family will never suffer hunger.

15th Generation: Grandfather Li Bing Lum

Hin Chew's son, Li Bing Lum was the first born in the Great House on September 24, 1881

There was a lot of pollical unrest in the village. Bandits were rampant and feared. It was in the 12th year of Emperor Kwong Shi when bandits first attacked killing our paternal uncle, number 2 son, as he was defending the great house on December 25th of that year. On January 5th, the whole band of bandits returned. They broke into many homes to pilfer. They forced their way in with lighted torches and swords. Having been there once before, they knew where to attack. what to do, what to steal, and who should die. They ransacked the property, injured the eye of Hin Chew and attacked his wife, Jao Shi, who was several months pregnant with her second child. She fiercely and frantically strove to protect both her unborn child as well as her three-year old son Bing Lum. Bing Lum was strapped to her back with a cloth carrier, she backed against a wall, creating a barrier between danger and her child. A blow from one of the bandit's swords had penetrated her thick winter clothes and wounded her in the right shoulder.

After the bandits had left, demolishing the house and scattering treasures everywhere, Hin Chew, Jao Shi and Bing Lum were alive. Hin Chew eventually healed from his wounds. Jao Shi carried her daughter to term, but the sword wound finally killed her in spite of care from many doctors in the region. She died on April 8th. Bing Lum, though only a small child, never forgot his mother for the sacrifice she made to save his life.

Bing Lum immigrated to America in 1909 at the age 28 on the basis of a "*Long time Califrn*" Li Bing Lum's wife Leung Oui Gei left Shanghai, China in 1917, boarded a Japanese vessel to America and arrived in San Francisco on April 26, 1917.

Li Bing Lum recorded a genealogical record of 17 generations of Li. The 17th generation consists of my Li cousins, one who is Stacy Li,

16th generation:
Gloria Li Chow

Written by Staci Li and Rodney Chow

I am not sure If Gloria, my mother, is the oldest of the Li family or is my Uncle John the oldest. She and my father are the beginning of what I know of the Chow family tree in America that began in 1927, the year she married my father.

On Monday December 8th, 1941, after the attack on Pearl Harbor, my mother's oldest brother, John, enlisted in the U.S. Army and was a Quarter Master Sergeant and fought in the South Pacific, New Guinea,

Guadalcanal and the Philippines. John was born in China. When America finally allowed the Chinese to become citizens of the United States, he and my mother were among the first foreign born Chinese to become an American Citizen.

Jonah, my mother's other brother graduated from the University of California Medical School in 1943. He was in the Army reserves in World War II. He practiced internal medicine and specialized in Hematology. For three years he was a researcher in nuclear medicine at the University of Oregon Medical School in Portland. UCSF medical school was impressed with his research and offered him a position of Associate Clinical Professor on their faculty. He both taught and had his private practice in San Francisco's Chinatown.

Joel my mother's youngest brother joined the U. S Army Air Force during World War II. He received his advance training at Randolf Field near San Antonio Texas. He was assigned to the 33rd fighter squadron within the Iceland command initially flying P-40 fighters for aerial escort of convoys and antisubmarine duties. After the war, he was a flying instructor in Oakland, California

On my father's side (the Chows) they were farm laborers and restaurant owner. My father left Hawaii in his late teens because he did not like working in the pineapple canneries. He settled in the Sacramento River Delta as a farm laborer and later as a share cropper growing Barlett pears in the early 1900's. He received his draft notice for military service in World War I, but the war ended before he reported for duty. So, he must have been in his late teens when he left Hawaii.

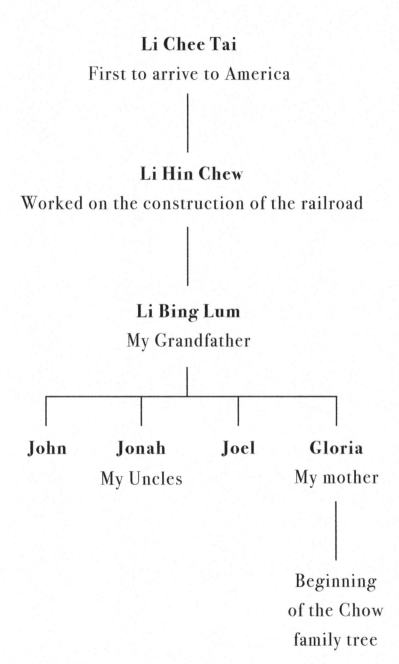

Li Chee Tai

First to arrive to America

Li Hin Chew

Worked on the construction of the railroad

Li Bing Lum

My Grandfather

John   **Jonah**   **Joel**   **Gloria**

My Uncles   My mother

Beginning
of the Chow
family tree

Uncle John – World War II

Uncle Joel – World War II

Chapter 1

THE BEGINNING

A BIOGRAPHY

I, Rodney H. Chow, am the fifth generation American on my mother's side, and the third generation from my father's side. I am descended from the early Chinese that lived along the Yangtze River that migrated south when times were bad and settled somewhere along the Pearl River upstream from Hong Kong.

On my mother's side, it started back in around 1812. A young teenage peasant was herding ducks near his home when some men from a merchant ship kidnapped him and made him work on their ship as a cabin boy. When the ship reached land in the Pacific Northwest where trees used for masts were plentiful, he jumped overboard and swam ashore. This was likely on the Oregon coast. He lived among the Indians and had a son. A few years later, he was able to return to China and then had a second wife and another son. One day, a soothsayer told him he must find his Indian wife and son, or he will have bad luck. So, he sent his son from his second wife on a quest to America to find them. He could not find them, but stayed in America and worked a variety of jobs. He was part of the Black Powder Gang blasting away the granite mountains for the building of the Central Pacific Railroad across the Sierras, in particular Cape Horn near the town of Colfax. He also dabbled in gold prospecting and fronting other prospectors' funds for mining supplies in return for a portion of their yield. He returned to China with sufficient funds to build a Great House. He is my maternal grandfather's father.

My grandfather on my father's side was among the Chinese recruited to work the fields in one of the Caribbean Islands. I do not know which. It was either Cuba or Jamaica. He later left the islands and worked his way across the United States and ended up in Hawaii. My father as a teenager worked in a pineapple cannery. He did not like the work, so he went to California to the town of Locke along the Sacramento River. He came to Locke because it was a town that was all Chinese and built by the Chinese that spoke his dialect. He became a sharecropper on an orchard growing Bartlett pears. In 1929, he lost everything. It was the beginning of the great depression. He came down to Los Angeles with my mother, sister and me, penniless and became a dishwasher in a restaurant. As soon as he saved enough money to buy an old used Ford pickup truck, he started his business peddling fish in neighborhoods where some Chinese lived.

The short stories in this book are based on my early years growing up when my father began his business. It is about the good side of life and the humor of a fifth generation Asian American.

Chapter 2

CHILDHOOD MEMORIES

CROCKER STREET

We had just moved to a two-story duplex on Crocker Street. The Lows lived upstairs while we were downstairs. It was 1936. That was the time when I first became aware of my surroundings. I was only seven years old. I had never given any thoughts to where we lived before coming to Crocker Street. I guess it was because of my young age and I had not experienced much to develop any attachments to any place. It was an idyllic world.

Grandpa, gosh he was an old man. He was almost fifty years old. I didn't see him as much as I heard about him, a legendary figure. He lived in Chinatown in San Francisco. Uncle John and Uncle Joel, both younger brothers of my mother, lived with us. Uncle Joel, the younger uncle, was still in high school. He attended John H. Francis Polytechnic High School on Washington Blvd. just past Grand Avenue. Uncle John, he sometimes lived with us for a week or a few months until he was able to find work.

Our lives centered on Crocker Street from Tenth Street to the midsection of our block. Those were the happy days; we didn't have a care in the world. We did not have the worries adults had about how to survive financially. There were two different worlds—the children's and the adults.

The street was our playground. Kick the Can, wow that was an exciting game. I took a chance and raced out to kick the can right after he counted to ten and was looking for anyone hiding. Although he was fifteen feet away, I was too slow. He got back to the can before I could kick it. Everyone laughed, and I became "it".

Rubber gun wars. We boys played cowboys by shooting at each other. Those were the days when automobiles tires were the slim ones with innertubes. Whenever the innertube got too many leaks for patches, it was discarded. The Awakawa boys who lived toward the southerly end of our street came up with the idea to cut the discards into half inch wide rubber bands—our ammunition!

Our block and the one across the street had a dirt alley. The alley on our block separated our homes from the commercial facilities that fronted San Pedro Street. There was a huge business for repairing or making wooden crates for holding farmer's vegetables. That was our source for discarded wood from which we made our play guns. The wood was the gun barrel. The local trash bin of the gas station on the corner of Crocker and Ninth Street was where we retrieved the discarded innertubes; it was our ammo dump. Then we attached a clothes pin taken from our mother's clothes line to the wood stick to serve as our trigger. The clothes pin held one end of the stretched rubber band on our wooded stick. Pressing down on that clothes pin released the tension in the stretched rubber band and the rubber band shot forward. Gosh, it was fun. We were laughing as we shot at each other with the rubber band that only traveled about four feet.

There were other forms of entertainment. When there was a nice soft wind, we flew our homemade kites. We took a discarded bamboo rake and cut the long bamboo handle into half inch strips then used tissue paper Mom saved from wrappings and the strings we bought at Joe's store on Ninth Street. Now, we had a kite which we flew together with other boys on our sidewalk.

Almost everyone had skates that we attached to our shoes for skating up and down the sidewalk of our block. When they got worn and ready for discarding, we took the skates and nailed them on to the half inch thick head board of a discarded fruit box. Then we nailed it onto another board to form an L shaped scooter that was braced with a small thin piece of the discarded fruit box. We had a home-made scooter 18" tall by 18" long.

Those were the carefree days. We were children playing together without any animosity towards each other. Oh yes, that was also when we came home from school shouting cuss words we picked up from the other boys. We didn't know they were bad words. It was fun calling each other by those names. Gosh, how embarrassed mom was when we surprised her with these newly learned fun words. We shouted these words when she least expected, in front of her and her friends. Mom was only in her late twenties. She grew up in a different era where children were tightly under control.

I do not remember any arguments or fights among us. Everyone, the boys and girls played together. We also had no awareness of being poor, even when there was a day when we did not have enough to eat. No one complained. I remember going to bed after having a dinner with soda crackers and water. Mom would soak the crackers in boiling water and add some soy sauce for extra flavor. That was dinner. Even though we were from ages eight to six, we somehow understood.

Some of our friends felt we were rich. Because we had something to eat most days. Actually, many times Pop could not sell all the fish he peddled. So, he cooked them for our dinner.

Whenever I wanted someone to play with, it was no problem. I just walked over to my friend's house and shouted. Robert! Robert! Then Robert would come out, and we somehow enjoyed each other's company playing whatever came to our minds. Robert lived on Tenth Street, just around the corner from us. His home was unique. The wooden garages in the back were built back-to-back from the garages on the other side of the block and side to side creating a rooftop of a playground for us.

Boy, was that neighbor mad when he saw us running over his garage roof. He was afraid we could cause leaks in his roof. It didn't stop us. He wasn't around all the time. Whenever he was, there were those angry words. Then we hurried away rushing back to Robert's yard.

I remember, Christmas was approaching in just a couple of days. One of our friends' family was so poor they could not celebrate Christmas like we did. My older sister asked Mom, "Can you give me some money to buy a tree for Nancy's family?" Mom took from what little she had for our meals and without a word handed the money to her. We felt so great, every one of us, even though we were not present when sister knocked on their door and handed the tree to them.

One day, it was just about dinner time. Robert's sister shouted from the front door, "Robert, time to eat!" Then she noticed I was with him, so, she said to me,

"Want to join us for dinner? You can have half of Robert's plate." You should have seen Robert's face. His eyes told me. You better not accept! I got the message and for self-preservation, said, "I am going home to eat."

Almost every kid would rush home at a certain hour before dinner and gather in front of the radio to listen to the adventures of the Lone Ranger and his faithful companion Tonto. The radio program started with the William Tell overture as the announcer spoke excitedly. I forgot the whole line, but it ended with "Hi Yo Silver, Away!" Every so often, a child could be seen singing the tune of the William Tell overture and galloping an imaginary horse, mimicking the Lone Ranger.

Our world was limited to three streets. We never thought of exploring the next street just one block away. They played with their friends just like we on our street. Those were the innocent childhood days, days, I enjoy reliving in my old age.

Sadly, though, all my friends are gone. The friendly street is no longer homes. It is a cold and uninviting—building after building of commercial buildings. A new generation of new immigrants now occupy those buildings with their small warehouses for their commercial goods.

Chapter 3

THE ATHLETE

I REMEMBER THOSE DAYS. I COULD NOT FIT IN WITH the boys no matter how I tried. There were other games though that did not require physical skills. One was "cut the Pie." Every boy had a pocket knife. It was a must-have gadget in every boy's pocket. The playground was dirt and was not paved like today's schoolyard. In the morning before class started, the boys played "cut the pie." A large circle was drawn on the ground, and we took out our pocket knives and with some skill threw them into the circle with the blade sticking in the ground. Then we drew a line from the center to the perimeter. Each boy had his turn, and the winner ended with the largest cut or as they called it the piece of pie. All that required was a skill for throwing the knife into the pie. I was good at that.

Another game was with marbles. We played Poison Hole where we used our thumb to shoot the marble into holes until we reached the last one and became the "poison one" that could knock off the others and caused them to be eliminated from the game. Every kid had marbles in their pockets. I remember some were much smaller than the standard ones and we called those the peewees. Then there was the much larger one we called the boulders. Poison Hole was played with standard sized marbles.

Well, physical strength was not important for these games and in those games, I fitted in quite well with the boys. But when it was kickball or baseball, no one wanted me on their team. Kickball and baseball were basically the same game except in kickball, the pitcher pitched the basketball size ball towards us only on the ground, and we kicked it and ran to the three bases like in baseball. I was smaller than the others and had not yet developed any athletic skills. I also did not have the physical strength the other boys had; I just did not fit in. I remember each class always had one hour of playtime that was supervised by a physical education instructor. Her name was Miss Butler. She made sure every child was included in the games.

The class voted for a captain and a team was made up by the boys from the class. She insisted that every boy had a chance to play on a team. When all the young athletes were chosen by the captain, I was never chosen. They knew I couldn't contribute anything to winning a game. No one wanted me on their team. I could not hold onto a ball that was thrown to me. They knew they had no chance of winning a game with me on their team.

Miss Butler did not see it that way. She demanded that one team included me. Gosh, you should have heard their disappointment when their team was forced to take me. "Aw, do we have to take him?"

I heard that complaint so many times. I wanted to be an asset for winning at least one game.

One baseball game, I got lucky. I made it to first base. I was so happy. My heart pounded with excitement. I could now show I could contribute to the team.

The next player came up to bat. He hit a homerun out of left field. I was on first and immediately ran for second and tripped on my clumsy legs. Oh! What a sad time. We lost the game. None of the boys wanted to talk to me. They were mad.

Another time, it was my turn to come up to bat. I was barely four feet tall. The other boys were at least six inches taller than me. I walked up to home plate and with both hands gripped the bat. I nervously waited for the pitcher to throw the ball to me. The baseball bat was about three feet long. It was almost as long as I was tall. As I was waiting for the pitch, I felt like I was holding a telephone pole. It was so huge and heavy. But I had to make a hit. The team depended on me. They were worried. If only some other kid would come up to bat instead of me. It was crucial for me to make it to first, so that the other boy on third could race home. The team needed just one more point to win the game.

Just as the pitcher threw the ball at me, at that split second moment, as I said to myself. "I got to hit that ball." With all my strength, I swung the bat at the ball. Never mind the bat I held was huge and heavy for someone so useless in a ball game. It took all my strength to swing my bat at the ball, but I missed.

"Strike one!" yelled the umpire.

I had two more chances to make good or I would be out. Oh! I was worried. They needed my run to win the game. The whole world was on my shoulders.

Just as the pitcher threw the ball, at that moment, as I was holding onto the bat, it felt like I was holding onto a bat so huge I could not hang onto. It was my last chance to make good. I swung my bat with all my might and not only missed the ball, but the bat slipped out of my grip and flew towards my teammates sitting on the bench! You should have seen the pandemonium as every boy tried to dodge the bat flying towards them.

It was the lowest time in my life. I could have hurt someone and there would have been no way I could apologize.

To this day, that was the highlight of my athletic career. The boys wanted nothing to do with me. Luckily the girls did not feel that way. They had a motherly instinct. But this was elementary school. Boys did not play with girls. The boys called me a sissy.

That's alright. Wait till they reached teenage. All of those boys will wish they had the attention I have with all the girls.

Chapter 4

MEMORIES

I REMEMBER THE TINY GROCERY STORE ON THE corner of Tenth and Crocker Street. The other little one across the street from this one, well, it did not feel like one of ours. Who knows why? Who cared? Maybe it was because they did not sell the ice cream bars on a stick where if you were lucky, you got one with the words "free stick." That meant the stick could be redeemed for a free one. The owner was the sole sales person. He also had the chocolate covered malt balls. There was one with a cherry inside. That was the lucky one. You got another chocolate covered malt ball if you got it.

Wonder Bread, Webster Bread and Olson were the only choices available to buy. Ten cents a loaf. Mom saved the bread wrapping for wrapping our sandwiches in our lunchboxes. Cream cheese came in a glass jar shaped and sized just right for cups. For breakfast, we toasted each slice of bread on a frying pan. Many times, we had to take a butter knife to scrap out the burnt portion of our toasted bread. When there was not enough money to buy jelly or a slice of baloney to make a sandwich, we dipped one side of the bread in sugar. That was a treat.

Several years later, probably around 1939, the economy improved a little to where we could enjoy a few more pleasures like buying pastries once in a while for breakfast. Those were the days when we walked along the South side of 10th Street at Town Avenue. We could smell the wonderful aroma from Ye Quality Bakery. Ye Quality was a wholesale bakery that cooked pastries like Apple Turnovers, Donuts and Danishes.

One of my favorite errands Mom had me do was going to Ye Quality to buy pastries for breakfast. Five cents for a donut. I liked the sugar one the most. Sometimes it was the twist. Apple turnover was great. I liked the fruit jelly in the center of the Danish. It made the Danish complete. I forgot what they cost. I am sure it was not more than 10 cents each.

Pet dogs roamed with their buddies just like we children. They knew when to come home every night. We saw the dogs mating; it was part of our natural surroundings, and no one paid attention. When the puppies were born, that was an occasion for us, just like when our parents had a new born child. We played with them until they were old enough to give away.

What I remember most vividly was the Toy Loan. Some charitable organization created a Toy Loan so we could play with toys we never dreamt existed. It was like a library. The children would select a toy and have it to play with for a week. Then return it so another child could play with it. Today thinking back to that time, we did not realize that we were that poor. There was no financial comparison amongst us to let us know how poor we were. Every family in our neighborhood was financially the same. We were satisfied with what we had and did not know there were more toys available.

There was another occasion I remembered. Someone from The Chinese Congregation Church took the children from our neighborhood to the church on Wilshire Blvd. We were told that the Wilshire Church had Christmas presents for us. I had anticipated a happy group of people would be there to hand each one of us a gift. When we arrived, there was only one person waiting for us. She let us into this large room with a huge Christmas tree with many toys under it. She told us to pick one toy to keep. Then without any ceremony we left. Although I was about eight or nine years old, I did not have the Christmas spirit from that occasion. I think a reception of friendly people would have made that an event more festive. But I did get a toy Mom and Pop could not afford to buy for me. That made me happy, and I played with it for quite some time.

Then there were times when the adults had their conversation amongst themselves. They had no idea I was listening. Everything I heard was like discovering something new. If they only realized what I heard them say was a learning event for me. They would suddenly wake up to see I understood them only as a child would with no experience to fully relate to what the subject was about.

The subject I remembered hearing was world politics. Communism was the current talk. I heard talk about the two different Russian political beliefs by referring to the Communist as Red and the other White. They often spoke about the Red Russians.

I was about seven or eight years old and I took every word I heard literally. One day a white stranger was in our neighborhood. Someone mentioned he was Russian. I looked at him and wondered why his skin was white instead of red. Didn't the adults say the Russians are Red?

Another time, a few of us were together, and one child mentioned we were the yellow race. The only color yellow we knew was that of a yellow crayon. We began to look on our arms and tried to find that shade of yellow on our skin. We looked and looked and couldn't find it.

Those were the days of innocence.

The one memory I have that is most precious to me was about a young White man who one day appeared in our neighborhood. He lived in another neighborhood. His name was Otto Zimmerman. He was like family to us. His profession was handyman. He came into our neighborhood with one purpose in mind. Bring the children to God. We children as well as adults loved him as if he was one of us. The Chinese community thought very highly of him. He enriched our lives to where our parents could not.

Our parents were accustomed to being confined to our neighborhood. They had learned not to venture out to places where eyes of hatred were cast on them. It was quite common for them to wait until they learned there was no animosity towards them will they go there to enjoy a day. Like spending a day at a particular beach or park. Otto being White did not have the fear of unpleasant encounters. He took us to places we were reluctant to visit, like the La Brea tar Pits. My favorite was Calico just a short distant from Barstow, California. That was before Calico became a popular ghost town for visitors.

Every Sunday morning, he would come to take us to the Free Methodist Church on Six Street. He sat with us during the Sunday School morning service. He used the Bible to teach us not to harbor bad feelings to those different from us.

That was many years ago. When I grew to adulthood. I still kept friendly relations with him even after I had a family. I would receive a postal card from him occasionally. Although he moved to Barstow, he still drove to Los Angeles once in a while to visit us.

He has passed on but the fond memories of him are forever.

Chapter 5

THE GOOD OLD DAYS

1940 WAS THE YEAR WE GOT A PEEK OF BETTER times. The Depression had eased a little. We were poor, but not as poor as a few years back. Pop's business grew from peddling fish from the large ice box he built on the back of his pickup truck to a store. That was the beginning of our slow climb upwards out of poverty. We could now afford to have a feast on special days.

You cannot imagine how often we celebrated. We had one huge advantage over most. We celebrated not only the American holidays, but also the special days from the culture of China. It seems like there was an excuse to have a special dinner almost every month. The American holidays we shared throughout the year were Easter, Fourth of July, Thanksgiving, Christmas and New Year. Yes! we must not forget the birthdays. Halloween? That was only for the youngsters. It was a costume day. No adults celebrated because the notion of adults in costumes was not yet an acceptable behavior

New Year Day is turkey, or baked ham with slices of pineapple and potato salad. Two weeks later, it was a birthday party for my sister. Then, somewhere, from January through February, it was the Chinese Lunar

New Year. The entire Chinese community would be enjoying the fire-crackers and the drummer beating the hell out of a huge drum with two heavy wooden clubs, about two inches in diameter and about two feet long. Another person was clanging the cymbals. They were drumming and clanging a rhythm for a teenager who was performing the lion dance over the exploding firecrackers. The lion dance depicted a lion that was awakened by the fire crackers. Thank goodness, the firecrackers were small and not so dangerous.

Somewhere from January through February after Chinese New Year, Pop cooked a Chinese feast for a special celebration carried over from China. We did not know for sure what it was for. Who cared? Pop knew, that's enough. It was the dinner that counted. Many times, it was a vegetarian dish. I remember it was a soup made mostly of fungus in the mushroom family. It could have been one of the Buddhist traditions. I am not sure how many other Chinese families did the same. It probably depended on how well one understood the value of a vegan dinner.

Next came March, my brother's birthday, another party for the children. Cake with candles was a must, so he could blow out the tiny candle flame. In April, it was Easter. Time to go to church to meet the pretty girls. Oh! Yes, and the church service. Then there was the Mid-Autumn Festival when moon cakes were a must. I could never remember which month it was. I just followed when the special mooncakes were being sold at our Chinese markets. I remember the mooncakes. They were about the size of a hamburger and made of some bean pastry with an egg yolk inside. So, when we cut it in half, it looked like the moon against the sky. Again, celebrating another day, we youngsters knew almost nothing about. But like always, it was the food that counted.

Before we knew, it was my birthday celebration. Then in June my younger sister's birthday. July Fourth came next. Every family had purchased fireworks and the neighborhood front yards were a display of beautiful colors of flame.

August was the month when the season was about to change to Fall. Then in late October the weather began to cool. That was when Pop will cook a special soup of water cress with a pork liver simmered till all the nourishment is in the soup. We drank the soup to build our immunity against sickness caused was the change in weather.

Not too long after that, Pop cooked anther vegan dinner to celebrate only he knew what for. We just loved his cooking.

Of course, the huge celebration was Thanksgiving. That is when the family comes together and feasted on turkey with all the trimmings. It was such a wonderful time. Everyone was enjoying the day together at the dinner table. I remember the conversations. It sounded like all the adults were talking and no one listening. We were so excited. The mashed potatoes with gravy and the delicious turkey stuffing were such a treat.

Before you knew it. Christmas was here, time to decorate the living room. Especially with the Christmas tree. Mom would place a sheet of cotton around the base of the tree to symbolize snow. The insides of our homes were one huge happiness. Then on Christmas morning, we rushed to the Christmas tree to open our gifts.

I remember that day vividly. Everyone, children as well as adults, unwrapping beautifully wrapped gifts. The excitement was throughout the living room where the Christmas tree was lit up with all the decorations on it. It was noisy, children playing with their new gifts or running around. Pop sat on his favorite couch enjoying the LA Times comics. I heard him mutter to himself.

"This is family!"

Not too long afterwards, it was December 31. I remember that was the day some neighbors would go out to a dark place in their yards and fire a few shots into the sky. That was the day they made sure their pistol still worked properly. But for we children, New Year started when we were sound asleep.

Chapter 6

MEMORIES OF
A BYGONE TIME

HOW ACCURATE IS THIS STORY? WHO KNOWS, I ONLY remember it from a Child's eyes. It was a culture unique to the neighborhood. I grew up in a neighborhood that practiced old world values mixed in with whatever could be gleaned from acquaintances that were part of what we saw as American. The mixture of old-world values with modern-day values was an interesting adventure I lived in.

The people in my neighborhood lived in two worlds. Neither one could be considered typical. The adults around me were struggling to survive in a culture that was neither Chinese nor American. They were bridging a social gap between the two cultures. The generation just before my time carried many of the values that were practiced in the villages back home in China. Yet they were heavily influenced by the dominant national culture by celebrating holidays such as Easter and the Fourth of July.

My father was of course the most influential for me. He belonged to a subculture that had not only American values from the 1930's but more significantly our local one which was a blend of every different ethnic culture on San Pedro Street.

There were popular phrases that were expressed during those days that are longer in use. I remember hearing my uncle's friends mentioning "wrong way Corrigan." I did not know he actually existed. I took it to mean doing something deliberately contrary to accepted mores. My father would use the word "hi-tone" to express his feeling of anything he deemed extraordinary or worthwhile. He used that term to describe something he could not afford, such as luxurious dinner ware or someone dressed in a new suit and tie, etc. Other times he muttered "Buda" referring to someone he did not like. For years while growing up, we wondered what he meant. It was not until many years later when I saw gang graffiti calling a competing gang "Putas" that I realize that it was a derived derogatory Hispanic reference.

Our neighborhood was a cauldron of different cultures blended together into a subculture germane to us. The older generation, particularly my parent's, looked upon my mine as unsophisticated in the correct behavior of their times. They could be heard saying, "These kids, all they know is hamburgers and chow mien." Back in those days, one greeting often said was, "Hey! Hong Yin". It was a friendly salutation to mean fellow Chinese. "Hong" as pronounced in the Say Yup dialect is "Tong" in the classic Cantonese. These are archaic terms when the Cantonese people did not speak Mandarin, the national northern Chinese language. Many times, instead of saying "Hong Yin," one would refer to each other as" Sai Goy," meaning little brother or youngster in Say Yup. They called China "Tong Saun." Cantonese words referring to the Ching Dynasty. The other word "saun" means mountain. To the best of my knowledge the word "saun" refers to a place. As an example, "Gum Saun "is Gold Mountain" for California. They heard stories that one could find gold herein California. So, it became "Gold Mountain." America was called "May Gwok," which means the beautiful country.

Whenever we wanted to describe a so-so restaurant, we called it a "greasy spoon." How about a town that is, well boring, not an exciting place. I remember hearing "they roll up their sidewalks at 6:00 PM."

When we saw someone, we had not seen for a couple of days, the greeting was "Where you been hiding?" an affectionate term expressing good friendship, meaning "I missed you."

"Andale and pronto," these were words borrowed from our Mexican neighbors, used by our mothers demanding the children to hurry up. Another borrowed expression we used was "eehola!" It was another Mexican expression like "Holy Smokes." The recollection of those expressions brings back happy childhood days on Crocker Street and San Pedro Street. Our streets, the home of our youth where our character and values evolved from the rich blend of all the different cultures in my neighborhood.

Chapter 7

SAN PEDRO STREET

THIS WAS A SPECIAL TIME AND PLACE IN MY LIFE.
The community that I knew from 1940 through 1947. We had moved
from Crocker Street to 9th Place just a half block from our fish and poultry
store. San Pedro Street was a half block away and is where we spent the
best time of our lives.

Pop and Mom were struggling to build their business. They divided
their store into two separate businesses, selling fish in one section and
poultry in the other one. While the Depression had eased up a little, times
were still bad, but not as disappointing as in previous years. Still, there
were days when hardly any customers come to buy.

Mom couldn't get to the store early because she was busy getting us
ready for school. Pop was already busy receiving fresh caught fish from
the fisherman who owned the fishing boats at the harbor. They were the
ones who caught the fish and delivered their catch themselves to save on
labor cost. The Market people were finished for the day and were now
relaxing at their favorite café. A few that walked past our fish and poultry
shop noticed the fish being unloaded onto Pop's cart from large boxes that
were two feet wide and four to five feet long, filled with fish with their gills

still moving. Those were the days when fresh meant fresh, not iced up on the showcase for many days.

Pop didn't even have time to push his loaded cart inside to stock up his showcase. The customers were already crowding around his boxes of fish, choosing and buying.

"Hey Joe! I want this one. I'll come back soon to pick it up."

To this day, I do not know how Pop kept track of which fish belonged to who. But he managed somehow. This was his busy time: he had to scale the fish and cut open the bellies, remove the guts and gills, then wrap the fish up for the customers, who then paid and took it home.

Some customers wanted a chicken. These were not cellophane wrapped chicken packages; they were live and had to be slaughtered, gutted, cleaned and wrapped, ready for pick up as soon possible. Pop had one hired laborer who did the slaughtering and cleaning.

Ten a.m.—Mom arrived. Thank goodness. Pop sure needed the help. She wrapped the gutted and cleaned chickens, labeled the packages with the names of the customer and the cost. The customers knew her, like an old friend. They paid her as she handed the wrapped chickens to them.

I remember the names of those that were not Chinese but a part of the lifeblood of our local economy. The one name everyone knew was Van Hout. He was the insurance person the Chinese had great respect for. He helped out in many ways besides selling insurance to our businesses. The Chinese looked to him for help in many situations unrelated to insurance that they did not understand.

Another one was Phil, a Jewish salesperson that sold supplies to the barber shops. Everyone knew him as a friend. Whenever he was on San Pedro Street, it was like seeing an old friend that belonged to us.

Then there was Charlie, a Black person who lived in an apartment just a half block away. He always came to visit us and many times when Pop was alone, he would watch the store so Pop could go get a cup of coffee.

Most of the friendly visits were from the local Chinese who would stop by and have a friendly chat with my mother. They spoke English fluently and were my mother's generation and had grown up some place in California. My mother had lots in common with them.

Then there were the men my father knew. They were the ones that would stop by our store to read the Chinese Newspaper Pop had saved for them. Many of these Chinese men were in their late 30's or early 40's. They were caught between two cultures. Their values were a hybrid between the old from China and modern-day America. I remember hearing a few frustratingly complaining. "I did not marry a Chinese woman; I married an American". They had discovered after they married that the second-generation young Chinese ladies were well educated and knew their rights. These newly married men could not rule the home the way their father had done.

I remember Pete. He was an emigrant from Germany. Then there was Harry. He came from Canada. Both of these men each supplied our store with live chickens for our store. They were not only a part of our community but were close friends with Pop.

Last of all, our pet dog Minnie. Back in those days, pet dogs were not looked upon as dangerous or a nuisance. They were just another part of our community that blended in unnoticed and not bothered by anyone. They just belonged. Minnie knew we were at the store, and every day, she would leave our back yard and come to our store to be with us. The customers knew her and never made much of an issue seeing her in our store.

In the afternoon, when the people from the city market had gone home, the casual customers from the neighborhood would come to chat or read the Chinese Newspapers Pop provided. Many of them lived just a block away in the same neighborhood. We were friends with common values. Our store was their social center.

A year later, World War II began. Many of our friends joined the military. Our medical doctor who had his medical office here joined up too. I was twelve years old. I did not notice the disappearance of so many of our local citizens. I didn't notice how young some of the recruits and local entrepreneurs were—military draft age and in their early twenties. It did not dawn on me how proud I should have felt about all these young citizens who somehow connected with us through our fish and poultry shop; most of them fought to save our homes.

I knew the war was on, and homes had hung up a small flag with a blue star to proudly show that a member of their family was fighting for us, but I just accepted life as it was presented to me. I saw how Mom and Pop adjusted with the booming business. I did not question it. I did not notice how life was changing.

Somehow, I have been given a valuable gift. I have been given an opportunity to witness a particular time when young people with a little money could start a business and survive. The entrepreneurs, the laborers, everyone from my neighborhood had a common goal in mind—to earn what little they could to survive the Great Depression. I saw them working ten hours a day, seven days of the week and saving as much as they could to send their children to college. They were not well educated, but they were young men who depended on no one except themselves. They were too proud to ask for help. Some were laborers, but many started a business at the bottom of the Depression. They were financially poor, but rich in determination and not afraid to gamble their last penny for a future of hope. These were the young men, in their late teens to early thirties, who made up our minority neighborhood. This was also when the great Depression began to disappear.

The young ones I have referred to are not the younger generation just ahead of me, but the older store keepers then in their early 40's. They were the ones that owned and operated the businesses on San Pedro Street. Many of them were either veterans of World War 1 or World War ll. They started their businesses, when they were in their early 20's.

Chapter 8

I WAS THERE

AS I LOOK BACK TO THOSE CHILDHOOD DAYS, I WAS starting from total innocence. I was like a sponge absorbing everything that was happening before me.

I remember the year 1938. It was Sunday. Everyone was home. Pop had a Ford panel truck the size of the small pickup trucks of that time. Uncle John was excited.

"There is a new car tire. It makes riding more comfortable. It is a balloon tire".

I didn't know it then, but it was the forerunner of the tires we have today, except it had a tube inside. Soon all the narrow ones would go into extinction. Uncle Joe had a Ford Coupe that allowed only one passenger and the driver. He had purchased his used car with the balloon tires. He exchanged the narrow ones on pops truck with the new balloon tires. What a big difference it made. Pop's truck suddenly looked modern. Uncle Joe placed pop's narrow tires onto his Ford coup and drove it for many years.

The following year, the auto industry started to place the headlights on front car fenders.

"I don't like it." said Uncle Joe. "It will cost more to replace the fenders if I have a wreck".

I was nine years old. Every word I heard from the adults was like learning something new. I shared their feelings with them. I was just being introduced to the world.

We had a dirt alley between the two rows of houses on each side of the block. I can still remember.

"Rags, bottles, sacks".

When we heard that chant, we took out what we did not want, and that man on his horse drawn wagon would give is a few pennies in exchange. It was a holdover business when transportation was by horses. That man and his horse were the last of that period. Not too long after, they disappeared.

On certain days, mom would place the empty milk bottles on the front porch before bed time. When we got up, the milk was sitting by the door for our breakfast. It was Adohr milk. The other milk was Carnation. But Adhor milk was from Guernsey cows. That made the difference. That slogan by Adhor worked miracles with us. Those days, the cream floated to the top, and one had to shake the bottle to blend it with the milk.

The ice man came on a certain day to deliver and place a block of ice into our icebox. While he carried the block of ice into our house, we children rushed to the back of his truck for the chips of ice we sucked on like candy. As time progressed, iceboxes were being replaced with refrigerators. It took me quite a few years to stop referring to our refrigerator as an icebox.

People were trying every way to earn a living. There was the organ grinder and his little monkey. He would stop by each house and grind his portable organ box. When we heard the music, we gathered around him and Mom would give us a penny for us to hand to his trained monkey.

It was fun watching the monkey take the penny and place it in his costume pocket.

Another vendor had a pony and a large box camera on a tripod. Mom paid a few cents to dress little brother in cowboy clothes and hat. Then he would take a photo of him sitting on the pony.

Times were beginning to improve to where Mom could afford to indulge us for a few cents.

During the hot summer days, someone with a large truck loaded with watermelons would drive slowly through our street and shout, "Water melons, water melons". Uncle Joe rushed out the door, ran up to the truck and asked, "How much?" Then he would say "Plug it". The man took out his knife and cut out a wedge-shaped plug of water melon for Uncle Joe to taste. Then that afternoon, all the children lifted a slice of the watermelon with two hands and bit into it. We spit the seeds out to where ever it was convenient.

The ice cream man pushed his walk behind cart that had dry ice to keep the ice cream from melting. He had bells on his handle and on front, a small heated box with Xlnt tamales for sale. That brand is still available in our super markets today. I forgot how much the ice cream cost. I think the hot tamale was twenty-five cents.

Some mornings, we noticed a homeless man had slept in our backyard. Mom would make him a peanut butter jelly sandwich and he would disappear. Those were the days when men broken in spirit with no means to earn a living were a part of our neighborhood. They lived in whatever shelter they were able to put together with discarded wood and cardboard boxes.

They were not a threat to our neighborhood, but they were also not a part of our culture. At times I visited with them. As I remember one time, one of these homeless men told me his sad story. They had lost everything in Oklahoma, and he had no job to earn a salary to support his family. He told me, it hurt him so badly seeing his family suffer from hunger. He could no longer face them. So, he left and ended up here in Los Angeles.

He was typical of many that were a casualty of the Great Depression.

I was only ten years old, but somehow, I felt his sadness. Years later, when I became a young adult and remembered this conversation, I had a different sadness hearing his story. I felt sorry for the family he abandoned.

Another time when I was about eleven or twelve-years old years old, I heard another sad story from another homeless person. He told me he was so poor that he did not have any means to help his sick wife. He started telling me how he stood by her bedside and watched her die. At that moment before he could say more, he broke down and cried. I was old enough to understand his emotion and felt very sorry for that man. Then one of the other homeless men scolded him for crying. I just stood there as he replied,

"I can't help it"

I remember the people in my neighborhood. They were too proud to beg on the street corners. They survived the best they could. There was no safety net in our neighborhood to help them. Every family was poor. Some more than others. Many of our people were either first or second generation in America. They were predominantly Asians, as well as White folks, Mexicans and a few Blacks.

This period ended beginning in 1942, when there were more jobs available then there were men and women looking for employment.

We were in the midst of World War II. San Pedro Street businesses were booming. Pop's fish business grew to wholesaling shrimp to restaurants. He finally reached his goal. He purchased his first house in 1943 for $4000.00 seller financed. In 1945, he built his two-story commercial building and proudly placed his name on it for all to see.

A few years later, supermarkets began to appear and the City Market began its decline. San Pedro Street was dying. Pop outlived his friends and neighbors. Many moved away. Their homes were being condemned by the city to achieve urban renewal. That move by the city created blocks of vacant lots. The neighborhood became a desert.

Mom hired an architect and lawyer to fight the city. She won by having the architect go to the old all white neighborhoods and photograph similar condition houses. Her lawyer then demanded the city condemn those homes along with our home. Her neighbors were not interested in joining her in her fight. They lost their home, and ours stood like a sore thumb, the only remaining house in a deserted neighborhood. The younger generation thought our home was a historical monument. It was not.

Mom died several years later. Pop became the only occupant. Homeless people filled his neighborhood. There was one business still alive. It was Modern Café. Pop's hangout where he joined the grandchildren of his friends for coffee and social life.

Pop was in his eighties. My sisters and brothers felt it was time for him to live in a better environment. So, we used his money to buy him into a senior condominium housing that was built by Chinese in the San Gabriel Valley. We thought he would enjoy the company of other senior Chinese. But these residents were new arrivals to America. They knew nothing about the Great Depression. He could not fit in. He grew up in a different culture from them. They had no interest in hearing him talk about his good old days. He also could not communicate in their language. He didn't understand one word they said unless it was in English. Fortunately, one of his neighbors spoke his dialect and could translate. That helped him socially.

His move was timely. Modern Café went out of business two years after he left the neighborhood. The commercial life on San Pedro Street had died.

Pop found a new interest during his daily walks—the hot dogs he liked at the 7/11 store. My sister tried to get him off the hot dogs for his health. But I told her,

"Let him enjoy the rest of his life the way he wants. He will soon be in his nineties. How many years will he saved by eating correctly?"

Pop lived to ninety-two.

Today, after years of neglect, a new resurgence appeared. San Pedro Street has been rebuilt. The street is now unrecognizable from the way it was during Pop's good old days.

As I looked back to those days long gone except for the nostalgic memories of my youth, I feel it was a wonderful life. A life I want to talk about to whoever I find that won't be bored to death listening to an old man from another time.

Chapter 9

IMPRESSIONS OF
A TEENAGER

I WAS AT THE AGE WHERE EVERYTHING WAS A DIS-
covery of life.

I was thirteen years old. At that time, I did not know what I know today. I remember those days. I saw the change on San Pedro Street. Our fish and poultry business suddenly came alive. Every morning before Pop opened his door for business, there was a long line of customers waiting.

I knew why. It was in the newspaper—stories of the War shortages and how industries were in full production twenty-four hours a day. I also saw it in the way our customers bought chickens and fish from us. The customers were no longer looking for the best price before buying what they needed. Red meat was rationed, and chicken and fish weren't. They bought whatever was available. Customers were coming from everywhere. Our business was not limited to our ethnic neighborhood.

Pete and Harry each had a business where they purchased chickens from farms in Los Angeles County and resold them to live poultry shops. Our store was one of the live poultry stores that depended on these two to help us meet the demand for chickens. Money was not as important for the customers as being able to have meat for dinner.

I saw it in the eyes of our customers. Anyone willing to work could get employment immediately. I saw a different outlook in my neighbors. Too poor to have the good life, they never dreamed of it before. Now, possibility was the feeling I saw on San Pedro Street. The harsh life of the Depression was over. Everyone was focused on the war. The wartime industries were taking anyone looking for employment. There were many openings and not enough people to fill the vacancies.

Crocker Street was residential. It was one block East and parallel to San Pedro Street. This was the street where I lived, before we moved to Ninth Place. Ninth Place was between Crocker Street and San Pedro Street. We were prepared for the expected enemy air raids. A warden was appointed to keep life organized in case enemy airplanes bombed our homes. An adult came to our school and told us how to stay safe from incendiary bombs. Information on how to recognize enemy airplanes was handed out to us. Stores were selling strips of tape that glowed in the dark for us to attach to stairs in case of blackouts. None of this made me feel any different. It was just what everyone did.

Several times, we heard the air raid sirens sound the alarm. The wardens were at the ready, and all lights were turned off. Then when the all-clear horns sounded, everyone continued life as if nothing unusual had happened. For me, this was part of the life I was learning from. Everything was new for me.

I remember Daylight Savings Time was established. The purpose was to save power for the wartime industries by using less electricity. It meant starting the day one hour earlier. Eight O'clock was actually seven. That was a change for me. Before, when I left in the morning for school, it was not as cold as it was now. The one hour made a difference to our comfort with weather. My friends and I stood in the sun to keep warm before class started.

One day, while I was walking to school with some friends, I heard a streetcar coming and saw it slow down. The driver kept clanging his bell and waved to us to get on. It was our gym teacher. I did not know he had a second job driving a streetcar before coming to Lafayette School to teach Gym. I had heard grownups talking about holding two jobs. Many men and women were doing it.

San Pedro Street at Ninth Street was where I either began walking along Ninth to go to downtown or board the yellow streetcar to go to school. The yellow streetcars were named by the alphabet. I took the S car, and when I reached Seventh and Broadway, I transferred to the J car to go to John Adams Jr. High. It cost me seven cents, and the transfer ticket was part of the fee to ride. Those were the days when anyone could travel almost anywhere in Los Angeles for seven cents.

Seventh Street and Broadway was the center of activities downtown. San Pedro Street from Ninth Street to past Tenth Street was our neighborhood shopping center. Broadway had the department stores, and San Pedro had the mom-and-Pop food businesses. The two very popular department stores on Broadway were May Company and Bullocks. May was about a block South of Seventh Street on Broadway, and Bullocks was North of Seventh Street. If I wanted something more reasonably priced, I went to the 5 and 10 cent Woolworth or Kress. Our neighborhood looked upon Bullocks as the upper end clothing store. If someone had enough wealth, they would walk to Hill Street to Robertsons. "Wow, you bought this from Robinsons!" someone would exclaim. Then there was Desmond Men and Boys clothing store on Broadway near Sixth Street. That is where I bought my trousers.

The sidewalks were crowded. There were so many people walking up and down Broadway. Seventh Street at Broadway was the center where it seemed everyone converged. That intersection was the busiest for boarding the yellow streetcars. There were so many people crowded in the safety zone to board them that the company had to have someone standing there to keep people under control for boarding. That intersection was also the popular Lowe's State Movie Theater. That was also where the truant officer could catch one or two kids skipping class to go to the movies.

The corner of San Pedro Street and Ninth was where we could board the yellow car. This is also where I saw the Redline. Redline was what we called the red streetcars. They were larger than the yellow cars and the size of a Pullman on the train. Many times, two would be linked together to make enough capacity to hold the commuters traveling between their homes in the suburbs and jobs downtown. I saw the sign on the car designating the destination for each Redline. One was Sierra Madre. I had no idea where Sierra Madre was located.

I knew Long Beach. My friends and I took the Redline to go there to spend the day at the beach. I remember when taking the Redline for Long Beach, we passed through a suburb called Watts. It was where White folks lived. The war industries had attracted so many from the South, that soon the Black neighborhood grew to surround Watts. It was a few years later when that entire area of Southern Los Angeles area became known as Watts.

Another time, my friend and I took the Redline to Santa Monica Beach. I had heard about Beverly Hills. I knew that city was where the rich lived. As the Redline drove along Santa Monica Boulevard, the car went through this city. I had never seen a street so beautifully landscaped.

I thought to myself, what a wonderful place this place must be to have a park all along the main thoroughfare.

The war ended in 1945. I was sixteen years old. The war time economy lasted only three years. I saw the beginning of a new era and the slow replacement of the old ways.

Supermarkets were the new shopping experience. The beginning of the end of prosperity for our fish and poultry business could be seen during Thanksgiving, Christmas, and New Year. That was when turkeys were a huge market draw. The supermarkets were selling these for the same prices Pop had to pay to buy from the local chicken farms.

The businesses on San Pedro Street could not keep up with the changes of the post War days, and soon they slowly died.

Looking back to those days, I do not feel there was much that could have been done about it. There was no way to survive against the supermarkets. I was eighteen years old. I knew Pop had an opportunity to seize a new success if he was willing to pioneer another minority business. But he was set in his ways and unwilling to change. So, progress left him behind.

Pop and Mom had successfully conquered the Great Depression. They were approaching retirement age and no longer had the will to fight and build, like when they were in the years of the 1940's.

Many of my generation went to college and settled in white collar careers. Those who returned to the old neighborhood were soon to see another opportunity, as newly arrived Asian immigrants began to replace the old.

Others like myself have entered the White world of the American Dream. Chinatown soon became a Southeast Asian community of Vietnamese, Thai, Burmese, etc. along with immigrants from Taiwan. The old community has grown with these new arrivals. The food there has also changed to the taste of the various Southeastern Asian cultures.

Although it has been enriched by the different regional cooking styles, it still has that Asian taste that I love.

Today, I am a stranger on San Pedro Street.

Time has changed, and although San Pedro Street no longer resembles the way it was in the old days I knew, I still have emotional ties with that part of Los Angeles. I feel like I am still a part of a community I no longer fit into.

Chapter 10

OUR HERO

YOU WOULD BE SURPRISED TO LEARN WHO WE admired as our hero. The grownups, what do they know. They had forgotten what life was about for an eight- to ten-year-old. But we will be kind and not be judgmental because they probably came from the horse and buggy world. They are so old fashioned. If they would only have listened to us when we boys were talking.

Johnny and three of his friends were doing some serious talk.

"Harry drove his father's pickup truck. I saw him alone behind the steering wheel."

"Wow!" Said Jimmie. "You mean he was really driving?"

"Yep! I saw him in that truck." said Johnny. "He drove the truck. The truck didn't drive him."

The conversation went on. Harry was doing something special. He was driving, and he did not have a driver's license. They knew they couldn't get a learner's driving permit until they were twelve. They also knew they couldn't get one unless their folks went to the Department of Motor Vehicle and got it for them.

Seeing Harry driving was what they wished they could also do. But their parents would never allow that. Maybe Harry had borrowed the keys to the truck without his father's or mother's knowledge. That thought was part of their conversation. Never the less he did it. He did what every boy wished he could do.

Jimmie exclaimed: "I sat on the driver's seat behind the steering wheel the other day. It was great. But I couldn't reach the gas pedal or brakes. Harry must have had some cushions on the seat behind him. I tried it, but I could only see through the steering wheel. I needed a cushion to lift me high enough to see through the windshield, but I could not reach the gas pedal."

Jimmie felt that Harry was the luckiest boy that ever lived. He could hardly wait until he became twelve years old. Then maybe Dad would help him get a learner's permit and teach him how to drive.

Jimmie and his friends knew the name of every car. Especially this year's models. The grownups were never a part of this interest. They were lucky just to own a used one. Only the rich guys could afford to buy a brand-new car. But at that age, the boys never gave any thought to how much it cost to own a car. They were not mature enough to know it cost money.

Older Brother had a hot rod. It had two exhaust pipes and whenever he lifted the hood to the engine, everyone crowded around the car to see the engine. They heard him talking to his friends. "I hit 60 miles per hour today." When Jimmie and his friends heard that, they felt like Older Brother was superman.

Whenever the older guys stood by to admire the souped-up engine, Jimmie and his friends joined in. All they saw was a silver painted engine with two carburetors. There was something special about it. And when they heard Brother talk about how fast he drove today. Wow! That was some achievement.

Jimmie and his friends saw in that engine the beauty as if another wiser person would admire some colorful flower. This momentarily satisfied their urge to drive a car.

Harry was their hero. He somehow got hold of his father's truck keys and drove the pickup truck without a driver's license. That took guts. If his dad had found out. Well, you know what could happen. He was fortunate that no police were there. Or he could have had a car accident, and his dad could hardly afford to pay for any damage. But these considerations never occurred to their minds. It was driving that mattered.

Yes, Harry did it, and all the boys wished they could have done the same. Harry was their hero.

So, there you are—four young boys who could hardly wait till they could live like the older boys they admired.

Chapter 11

SUNDAY WITH
MY GODFATHER

EVERY SUNDAY, MY GODFATHER, CAME TO PICK ME up in his little truck. He had a 30-acre farm in Artesia. I remembered it was an asparagus farm on the southwest corner of Norwalk Blvd and Del Amo.

He was a man of many interests. The farm was just a side venture. His principle business was a noodle factory in town that supplied the Chinese restaurants in Chinatown and other outlying areas. I remember Lee, who managed the farm for him. He did not have a tractor; he only had a horse to pull the plow. That horse had a mind of his own. He decided when pulling the plow was over, it was time to return to the barn. That was when Lee could not fully control the horse. I saw the horse racing back to the barn with Lee almost running and barely able to hang onto the plow, frantically shouting, "Whoa, whoa!". That was really something to see.

I was left alone to enjoy myself on the farm. There were horned toads everywhere. I sometimes caught one and played with it until it was time to go home. There was so much to enjoy on the farm for someone like me that only knew Crocker Street and my urban friends nearby. I have always loved the smell of fresh air on the farm. I thought it was amazing that the air was so refreshing. I was so accustomed to the smell of the live poultry in Pop's store that that unusual aroma never bothered me. I thought that was normal city air.

There were times when some lady came to our store to buy a chicken. I saw her pinching her nose and thought to myself. "What is she so snobbish about. Is she trying to tell us she is better than us?" It never dawned on me. The sweet smell of the country air was not because it was where open fields existed. It smelled so good because I was so habituated to the bad odor from the chickens that I never realized that was not the norm.

When the season for asparagus was about to be over, Lee would stop harvesting the shoots for the market and let the plants grow to bushes. He waited until the bushes grew to maturity then he would cut and safely burn them. This was the dormant time for the asparagus plants.

Those were the Sundays I enjoyed the most. It was when the fields were clear of the dying bushes and the ground was plowed and prepared for the resurgence of the asparagus. It was an open field with no plants growing. But not devoid of any life. Throughout the prepared ground would be the nest the birds built. I saw the tiny eggs in the nest. The next Sunday, I went out into the field to see the nest and saw it empty. Lee told me the baby birds had hatched out and did not require too many days to grew strong enough to fly away with the older birds. I was amazed at this short interval needed for the birds to grow from helpless chicks to birds that flew. I wished I was around when the birds flew away. It must have been quite a spectacle to see mother nature at her height.

When the asparagus bushes filled the field with green, larger birds began to nest there. I saw them. They looked like pheasants. Lee constantly had to confront bird hunters with their shot guns and tell them to leave.

He told them they could mistakenly shoot a farm worker among the tall asparagus bushes.

I remember riding in the truck with my Godfather as he drove out to the countryside to talk with Lee about the farm. Those were the years when the Los Angeles city urban houses ended at Soto Street. The landmark for this perceived boundary was the huge Sears store on Olympic Blvd. The stockyards for cattle were not too far away from these homes. Another landmark was the beautiful architecture of this large commercial complex. It resembled a fortress from ancient Greek mythology. I am so glad the owners of that beautiful structure have preserved it and kept it as a front for the shopping mall they built behind.

There was a small air field on Pioneer Blvd. not too many miles along Olympic Blvd. The landing strip was a graded dirt runway for the light Piper Cubs that flew in and out of that field. I remember seeing one hangar and a wind sock. I believe this little-known small craft landing field was in Downey or very close to it.

Artesia was such a nice community. Today TV programs depict small towns like this for stories of a simple life that no longer exists. Artesia has been absorbed into the mainstream urban living. Sadly, I hear the locals today pronounce the street where the asparagus farm was as "De Lamo". We pronounced it then as "Del Amo".

When Godfather drove along Pioneer Blvd. through the town of Artesia, I was fascinated with the scenery of the countryside. It must also have been a very happy time for him. He loved to tell me stories of his youth before he married. Especially how he miraculously survived the near accidents from his driving. As he told me those stories, he would laugh loudly enjoying the attention I gave him. Other times, he would be humming the tunes he remembered from the church service back when he attended church service.

He was a good cook. I remember the chow mein he cooked for our lunch. It was different from the way my father cooked it, and it was delicious. After lunch, he always stopped at the drug store in Artesia. There was a large soda fountain counter, and we would have either a milkshake or a malt.

That was my Sunday that I remember so fondly. I was twelve years old.

Chapter 12

WATTS RIOT

ONE DAY, A POLICEMAN STOPPED A BLACK PERSON for some traffic violation. This happened in Watts, where most Black people lived. It was well known that the freedom to live wherever one could afford was denied to all minorities. Los Angeles was a place where invisible boundaries separated each racial group. There was a common knowledge that the good opportunities were restricted to White folks. This created an underlying resentment that was hidden in the hearts of many minorities. They wanted to belong and be treated with dignity. The feeling of being looked down upon was the powder keg that could easily explode in violence. This traffic violation and subsequent citing by a White policeman lit the short fuse to this pent-up anger.

I was about ten miles away from where this incident occurred. I saw the smoke rising in the sky. People were excitedly shouting. "There is a riot over there."

Although the business district where I stood was at a safe distant away, everyone was worried it could spill to this area. Luckily that did not happen.

I was carried away by the same question many had. "What is going on? Why are they rioting?"

Although I did not have the opportunities the White folks took for granted, my people were able to build an economy that allowed us to live comfortably. We, however, like the Black community wanted to be accepted with dignity. We wanted to belong, although we were not able to reach what we yearned for. We did achieve some success that was hard earned. That was why it was difficult for me to understand why anyone would destroy what little they had in a riot.

This was in the 1960's. The newspapers called it the Watts Riot. Most people had a comfortable life with a future ahead if they wanted it. But unfortunately, there was this very large community whose opportunities were extremely limited.

The Blacks had no intimate feelings for the businesses they set fire to because they did not see them as part of their community. The underlying feeling was these businesses took from them and gave nothing back.

As I was discussing this event with my co-workers, I, like many others had come to a conclusion without first considering the facts. My thoughts were why would anyone destroy their livelihood, the businesses where they purchased their daily needs?

I did not give any consideration to why these people rioted until the next day at work. Comments were made by some who had no idea what a Black community had to endure. I joined them in their assessment of the cost to that community. I made similar remarks.

"They are destroying their local economy that they depend on for daily living. It sure doesn't make sense."

I knew several Black co-workers in my work place. These Black friends knew they were prevented to rise above to more responsible positions. They came from a community that was treated unfairly as in a caste system. That morning after the Watts Riots, I heard their comments. Those buildings, the stores where they shopped did not belong to them. Then it became apparent that they felt they have been kept out of reach of that part of the economy. They were kept suppressed by the poor schooling in their neighborhood, and as adults were prevented from rising to the responsibilities the ordinary White folks took for granted. There was no future for them. So, they let out their frustration by burning and destroying what they perceived they could never have.

Some of the Black men began to speak up, and many listened. I was one of them. It began to impress me, especially when they exclaimed. "We do not want you to tolerate us. We want to be part of your life. Do not just laugh at our jokes, laugh with us."

This event exposed me to a very important learning event. I began to understand humanity. I learned that the most important lesson of my life was not the Watts Riot but how my Black co-workers felt. Then I realized the most precious gift one can give to another can be said in one word—RESPECT.

Now that I am in my twilight years, I am re-evaluating the history of my life. I have come to realize that the road I traveled was filled with opportunities that were made possible through the efforts of the Black movement for equal treatment.

Hopefully there are enough of us who understand that God created everyone to be treated equally. Perhaps then, we could be the beacon for our younger generations to follow.

Chapter 13

GREAT OAK TREES COME FROM LITTLE ACORNS

YES, THEY DO. BUT THEY CANNOT GROW WITHOUT natures help. A good head start will help.

When I left Lafayette Jr. High and transferred to John Adams, I was far behind the students who were well prepared for the math and English classes. My classmates had the training in grammar as simple as identifying a noun and a verb. They had the lessons for the basic concept for writing and were ready to continue on to the next higher level of English. I was in class with them at John Adams, trying to understand the teacher while the others were able to move ahead because they already knew what I did not know. I spent valuable time struggling to keep up with them. It was because I came from a school that had low standards and the teachers did not give their students the opportunity to build a good foundation to advance.

Of course, how successful a child can be has a lot to do with his or her innate intelligence. But even though that is an important consideration, isn't it a shame to prejudge a child's capability and deprive them of a future by not showing them what opportunities exist? I am referring to the schools in neighborhoods where parents are demanding bussing for their children to escape the poor attitude that their children are not capable for with higher learning. It would be helpful to have a public relations person from industry come to show these students the careers available to them. Perhaps then the students would have a target to achieve and a will to drive their school to higher standards.

What I am trying to say is, not every child has the mentoring they need to lead them have more choices. This is where the schools can help by showing our young generation there are fields of opportunity they have not been exposed to. Opportunities that require the education of our sciences, such as physics, mathematics and chemistry.

Chapter 14

LIFE IS A LEARNING EVENT

LIFE HAS BEEN A CONTINUOUS LEARNING EVENT.
Not all that I learned happened by how I lived. Much of it I witnessed was from afar. It was the protest by our youth that redirected our lives for a better world.

I saw three very important happenings in my life time. These happenings forced society to change for better times. The first was the Zoot Suit era. The second was the mass migrations that brought different people together for one cause—the wars, and the third was the hippies.

I had graduated from elementary school to jr. high when many of the youths from poorer neighborhoods wore their symbol of protest. They wanted respect and acceptance instead of being looked down as undesirables. They dressed in a style different from the norm to show their pride and independence. Although many of the Zoot Suiters were only conforming to the local majority. They wanted to belong and not be an outsider among their own kind. They all had one objective in their mind. They wanted the world to know, it is my life, the way I want to live. I am sure that was the reason for their in-your-face attitude. However, I believe their outlandish dress code hid the true motive in their hearts. It was a cry for a share of the opportunities they saw the White world had.

I saw the reaction from those they wanted to be a part of. These were the ones who knew how fragile their good life was and they were afraid to lose any portion of it. Their greatest fear was losing their hard earn position in the decision world to those they believe were inferior. Deep in their hearts were also a fear of being treated like they have treated the less privileged.

This happened in around 1940 through 1943. The end for the Zoot Suiters came violently. The men in military uniform were not impressed and saw these Zoot Suiters as rebels against society. These Zoot Suiters were humiliated by being over powered in numbers and were stripped of their clothing in public. The military draft for the War effort finished off this era, and that period died as suddenly as it appeared.

This era was too short to make an impact on our way of life.

I saw the second great shift in attitude. World War II caused it. There was a great effort to unite everyone to fight the enemy. Songs sent messages to unite everyone and say that despite our ethnic differences, we were all Americans. I believe the most effective cause for bringing everyone to feel like they belonged came about when everyone had one thing in common. They had to work together to fight the enemy. When they shared the same goals, they began to notice cultures different from what they knew. Especially when they tasted the cuisine. Everyone began to discover through ethnic restaurants, the richness each different culture contributes to make our lives more interesting.

The third event I saw came after the War. The youth of America saw a culture that was not opened to change. They were protesting the rigidity of the establishment and wanted a more liberal attitude towards everyone. Like the Zoot Suiters of time past, they had the same in-your-face attitude.

They challenged the norm with their back to the Earth life style and created a living habit away from the artificial manufactured conveniences taking over our lives. At the beginning of this period, their kind was the youth who wanted to save the environment. A few began to listen to them and began to question: What are we doing to our Earth?

Like the Zoot Suiters, they were not looked at with any great kindness. It was because of their carefree attitude, the way they dressed and especially their appearance that did not conform to the norm.

It has taken more than a decade for this thinking to influence how we could save this fragile earth. Up to this time, we unknowingly have been our own enemies. Now our focus is on how our food is grown.

I believe we are now beginning to profit from the message these young hippies were trying to tell us in the movement towards organic farming, or at least eating our food free from the residual toxic pest control used for increasing yields.

This young generation began to grow crops organically for their own consumption. Soon, the general public caught on, and farmers markets were born and became the source for healthy grown food. The popularity of this movement differed from earlier ones because it had what everyone wants—a better and healthier life.

The world has awakened to the message. They began to offer organic foods in the supermarkets. They are also trying to join farmers market for the profit. Today it is a constant effort to preserve farmers markets for the little guy who otherwise would find it difficult to grow their family businesses.

I am now 94 years old. I have lived through the years of the 1940's to the present, and I have seen the hidden emotions that made everyone either comfortable or uncomfortable. It seems that all people bond together only when they enjoy the same outlook in life. It is when the establishment wanted what the hippies tried to tell them that they began to realize there are no threats to their fragile existence. This group of youth may not fit the norm. They are only demanding a space for freedom of expression. The voices of this minority shouts at the majority by the way they behave and look. It is not until enough people discovers that these youth see something they have overlooked. It is not until most everyone begins to embraces these new ideas and accept it as part of their culture, that these youth begin to receive what they have always wanted—being accepted and respected for being outspoken and an independent thinkers.

Chapter 15

DO YOU REMEMBER

THAT WAS THE DAY THAT TESTED OUR BRAVERY.
We were 16 years old in the prime of our lives. Come on now, you guys.
Do you remember when you finally got enough courage to approach
that lovely girl and ask her to go to the school dance with you? Up to that
time, we were on safe ground. We were with the guys enjoying football or
basketball. Everyone was interested in the same thing. There was never
any thought of "Will I fit in?"

Do you remember those high school days? We were not the Don
Juans that could charm the girls. Johnny was as smooth as silk. We noticed
how at ease he was with the girls. It seemed like all the girls wanted to
be escorted to the school dance with him. But for the rest of us, we were
walking on thin ice, never knowing if we were to make a stupid misstep
and be the one the girls might think, that "He is a jerk." But those of us, not
the Don Juans, that was a bridge we had to cross. It was our rite of passage.

The school dance was the highlight of our social activity. The girls
knew how to dance with a partner. We had to have a crash course to learn
from big sister. What scared us to death was making a fool of ourselves.
Will she say yes? Gosh, this is a different kind of bravery. It had everything

to do with our self-confidence and she was the one that would make or break our self-esteem.

All the other guys had no trouble getting a date. The girls all wanted to be with them. Scared as we were, we had to cross that bridge. So, we approached her when she was alone. It was less embarrassing if she said no and no one was there to witness the rejection.

She seemed so confident. She was in the driver's seat. You did not have a chance. She is the one who said yes or no. She knew everything about you. Girls talk, you know. The guys, well they are not as macho as one would think. Doing physical work was easy. It only took strength. But asking a girl for a date? Especially the first time in your life? It takes courage. Sad to admit, we guys are cowards.

We were at the doorstep of the unknown. There was no way out, if we want to join the fun at the dance. We just had to summon up enough courage to walk up to her and ask. She said, "*Yes. I would love to go with you.*" Wow, what a feeling. It was like walking in midair. Just imagine how proud we were when we entered the ballroom holding the hand of the prettiest girl in school

Chapter 16

JOE KINDA

I REMEMBER WHEN I FIRST MET JOE KINDA. IT WAS
1943. I wanted an education that I could not receive in Lafayette. So, I
transferred to John Adams Jr. High. I did not know anyone because I did
not live within the school boundary for John Adams. It was during lunch
period when I met new friends. They were all friendly, nothing unusual
except for this one boy. Just another boy that I happened to meet. He
loved to tell the stories he heard from his father. I was very interested
in the stories about his father's life in Hungary. He told me what he had
learned from his father about the Magyars. Joe was very proud of his
Hungarian background, particularly the Magyars who are the ancestors
of modern-day Hungarians.

I have always loved history, especially about the origins of different
people. I was fascinated listening to him as he told me the Magyars came
from some place between Mongolia and Tibet adjacent to China. The
stories I loved to hear the most were about his father's life before he left
Hungary to come to America.

Although Joe's heritage was from Europe and mine was from Asia, I
discovered similarities about his childhood with mine. Although I am the

fifth generation in America and Joe was the second generation, I, like Joe am bilingual. I do not remember which language I learned first—Chinese or English. Joe spoke Hungarian before he knew English. We both grew up in our particular ethnic neighborhood. Mine was in Los Angeles, and Joe's was from one of the states in the Midwest. It was through him during my high school years, that I learned to appreciate there are other people, who are White, who also came from a cultural background different from mainstream American.

Joe was a very kind and considerate person. That and the interesting stories he told me were the glue that bonded us together in friendship that began when we were thirteen years old and continued through our high school days.

Joe and I graduated to John H. Francis Polytechnic High school on Washington Blvd. just off the corner of Grand Avenue. Then we met again. This time it was in the surveying class taught by a former land surveyor who changed his career to high school teaching. It was during that class that we became close friends. Joe and I spent many lunch times together. He was the one who talked me into joining the wrestling tournament held during lunch break.

I have always kidded Joe about how he became the champion wrestler and I lost every bout. Joe never liked to brag, so he would just ignore me whenever I started to laugh about it.

Joe had an old used Plymouth sedan, and whenever he had enough money for gas, he and I took rides in it. Those were the good old days I had with Joe.

Hal was a classmate in our surveying class. This was the heyday of hotrods. That is what we called the old cars the boys converted into their version of a race car. Hal did not have enough money to complete his hotrod. It was a Model B Ford roadster that formerly had a removable canvas top. He did not have enough money to rebuild the brakes. So, he drove very slowly and shifted to reverse to stop the car. Each time hoping, he did not damage the gears in the transmission box. Joe and I were his passengers as we drove past the other students walking as school let out. It was fun as Joe and I shouted, "No brakes! No brakes!" warning everyone to stay safe and not get hit by Hal's hot rod.

World War II ended in 1945, and the wartime economy was winding down. Even though we were no longer in the Depression. Joe still delivered newspapers in the morning before school started.

After school let out, Joe stayed and practiced for the high school team. I had to go to Chinese language school.

Back in 1947 when both Joe and I were in our senior year, Joe told me that there are very few families with the name Kinda. So, If I wanted to find him, just look up the name Kinda in the telephone book, and that Kinda would most likely be him or a member of his family.

After graduation from high school both Joe and I went separate ways. We had no contact with each other for about ten years. Then one evening, I began to recall the good times I had with Joe. I remember what he told me on how to find him. So, I opened the telephone book and found a Kinda. I immediately dialed that number and introduced myself and asked if they knew Joe. The person on the telephone was Joe's sister-in-law. She immediately gave me joe's telephone number.

I did not know that Joe's sister-in-law had immediately called Joe's wife Pat. When I dialed Joe's number, a lady answered. She said, "Joe does not want to talk to anyone after work. He needs the rest. But I am going to disturb him."

She sounded very excited because their sister-in-law had reached her before I did and told her I would be calling.

That was how we reconnected and resumed our friendship. Every year after, Joe and I would fly to the Northwest Territory of Canada and spend one week fishing. Many times, we would just relax in our fishing boat without saying a word to each other. We were so close that it seemed we were mentally in the same wave length.

Our friendship was like two brothers with a very close bond. We thought alike and our values were the same. Joe is the closest friend I have had.

I never dreamed that our friendship would last a lifetime, especially with someone from outside of my neighborhood. This is America, the melting pot of people from different parts of the world. It is an awakening that if we give life a chance, good things can surface and we can learn to respect others who are different than those we are familiar with.

Both Joe and I are 93 years old. I will be 94 in May and two weeks later in June, Joe would have been 94.

Life time old buddies.
We met when we were thirteen years old. Left to
right: Rodney Chow, Lucky Godwin, Joe Kinda

Chapter 17

IT HAS BEEN A GOOD LIFE

ON MAY 27, 1983 IN THE AFTERNOON, I WAS AT MY construction site in Palmdale. Joe and Lucky walked towards me. What a wonderful surprise. They drove all the way from Los Angeles with a sheet cake for my birthday. I do not know who felt the best. Joe and Lucky or me. I got a surprise birthday party, just the three of us. We have been friends since we were thirteen years old. We were all the same age, 54 years old. They took their valuable time to make me happy.

It was the three of us. Lifetime buddies from when we met in John Adams Jr. High. Lucky died a few years later. Joe and I continue to enjoy each other's company going fishing every year to either Alaska, Canada or the state of Utah.

Every year Jim, whom Joe knew, would organize a fishing trip to Canada or Alaska. Jim made sure it was when the ice and snow melted. Great Bear Lake was the destination where we roughed it in the wilds. Roughing it? Well, it was in the Arctic, in the North West Territories of Canada. It was a lodge with all the comforts of a ritzy hotel. There was no radio, no television, just a man's world where fishing was the topic each day.

I remember those trips we made every year. Joe and I would fly to Edmonton, Canada, where everyone would come and wait for the private plane from the lodge to take us to the lodge at Great Bear Lake. There were 16 of us, all old fishing friends that Jim had organized for this fishing trip.

Vern, one of our fishing friends kept every moment alive with his jokes. I remember when the plane began its descent on the landing field. Vern was pouring mosquito repellent on his arms and jokingly proclaimed, "I am using enough repellent so when the mosquitoes try to land on me, they will just slide off my arm." Then I saw the swarms of mosquitoes, thousands flying around.

After supper, we relaxed in the social room. Some playing poker, some just enjoying each other in conversation. But the most amazing activity I saw was the guys watching the fishing videos. You could hear the men shouting, "Wow! What a fight it took to land that fish." They never got tired of watching one catch after another.

The lodge was a catch and release resort. That was a conservation act to not deplete the lake of the large fish. All we were allowed to do was cast our line out, catch the fish, and reel the fish to our boat. Then the Indian guide would carefully take the hook off the fish, and revive it before releasing the fish back to the wilds.

Fishing with my friends was just one week in the summer. Joe and the others had a business that needed attention. I was retired and had planted apple trees on five acres. I needed something to keep me busy while waiting for the trees to mature and produce fruit. So, I decided to become a real estate sales person. I never imagined when I joined the real estate office of Patterson and Tintorri that it would lead me to another very close friendship. This time with Pat Patterson, the owner of that brokerage.

Talking about the good old days, about my life with my lifelong friends. That's what I like to do. Especially, talking about it to anyone who wouldn't mind listening to a 94-year-old codger like me. Sharing that good life with anyone that might be interested, is what growing old gracefully is all about.

EPILOGUE

HOPEFULLY, WHEN THESE STORIES ARE READ, ONE will get the feeling that their childhood days were no different than those in ethnic neighborhoods. The stories in this book are meant to show that immigrants to America have much in common with all Americans.

Although one's back ground may not fit the history we are taught during our early childhood days, as we become a part of mainstream America, we are influencing the established culture to become richer with what our families brought with them when they came to this country.

I have taken you on a journey that hopefully will remind you of your good old days. I tried to portray a life that existed during the Great Depression and what we experienced from the 1930's through the 1970's. I want this book of short stories to show everyone that our path to the good life is the same no matter what is our origin.

The best days of our lives are

when we were young

All there was to live for was eat and play

No need to worry about another day

Mom and Pop took care of that

Soon we will discover

What a wonderful life we can have

if we give life a chance

Good things can surface

Especially when we learn to respect

Those who are different

From those we know